Now all the luggage was loaded into the hold of the aircraft, except of course the one that said BY HAND OF PILOT, which was taken to the cockpit. And so when the jumbo jet took off from the airport, neither the pilot nor the co-pilot knew that, stuck on the clamped neck of the diplomatic bag beside them, was a British snail, who, though he did not know it, was travelling to America!

Titles available by Dick King-Smith, award-winning
author and creator of *Babe*:

Published by Corgi Pups
HAPPY MOUSEDAY

Published by Doubleday/Young Corgi
THE ADVENTUROUS SNAIL
ALL BECAUSE OF JACKSON
BILLY THE BIRD
THE CATLADY
CONNIE AND ROLLO
E.S.P.
FUNNY FRANK
THE GUARD DOG
HORSE PIE
OMNIBOMBULATOR
TITUS RULES OK!

Published by Doubleday/Corgi Yearling
A MOUSE CALLED WOLF
HARRIET'S HARE
MR APE

Published by Corgi
THE CROWSTARVER
GODHANGER

THE
ADVENTUROUS
SNAIL

DICK KING-SMITH

Illustrated by John Eastwood

THE ADVENTUROUS SNAIL
A YOUNG CORGI BOOK : 0 552 55390 5

First published in Great Britain by Doubleday,
an imprint of Random House Children's Books

Doubleday edition published 2003
Young Corgi edition published 2004

Set in 16/20pt Bembo Schoolbook

Young Corgi Books are published by Random House Children's Books,
61–63 Uxbridge Road, London W5 5SA,
a division of The Random House Group Ltd,
in Australia by Random House Australia (Pty) Ltd,
20 Alfred Street, Milsons Point, Sydney, NSW 2061, Australia,
in New Zealand by Random House New Zealand Ltd,
18 Poland Road, Glenfield, Auckland 10, New Zealand,
and in South Africa by Random House (Pty) Ltd,
Isle of Houghton, Corner of Boundary Road & Carse O'Gowrie,
Houghton 2198, South Africa.

THE RANDOM HOUSE GROUP Limited Reg. No. 954009
www.kidsatrandomhouse.co.uk

A CIP catalogue record for this book is available from the British Library.

Printed and bound in Great Britain by
Cox & Wyman Ltd, Reading, Berkshire.

Chapter One

Like all snails, Siegfried moved very slowly.

Unlike any other snail, he was adventurous.

Like many adventurers, he sometimes did rather foolish things. Like boarding an aeroplane.

Siegfried lived in some rough grass at the edge of one of the runways of a large airport. Deep in the grass, he could not see the aircraft that landed or took off close to his home patch, but he could hear them all right.

Often he thought he would like to have a look at whatever was making such a noise, every ten minutes or so, every hour of every day. He was curious, which is part of being adventurous, and so early one fine sunny morning, he slid out of the grass on to the tarmac of the runway and set off to see what he could find. After an hour Siegfried had travelled about two metres, and by the afternoon he'd reached the middle of the runway.

The bursts of noise were much louder now and the ground shook under his foot (which is what the underneath of a snail is called).

Suddenly there was a terrible blast of sound, very very close, which made Siegfried stop in his tracks. This was just as well, for one of the huge wheels of a newly-landed aeroplane went whizzing past him, missing him by a fraction.

"What was that?" said curious Siegfried (he talked to himself a good deal).

"I don't know but I'll find out," said adventurous Siegfried, and he turned to follow the direction in which the noise had gone, his slimy trail glistening behind him in the sunshine. Luckily for Siegfried – you need luck if you're adventurous – the aircraft had turned and taxied back towards him before finally stopping for its passengers to disembark, so that it only took the snail another couple of hours to reach it.

In fact he reached one of its wheels, the one on the opposite side to the wheel that had so nearly squashed him. He did not know that it was a wheel. He did not know that the rubber mountain he now set out to climb was a tyre.

He only knew that he was determined – as all adventurers must be – to find out more.

Very slowly, Siegfried began to climb. He climbed around one side of the tyre, then over the top of it, then down the other side to the ground again, just where he'd started an hour ago. Right round the wheel was a trail of sticky slime.

Goodness knows how many times adventurous, curious, determined Siegfried might have gone round that aircraft wheel on his sticky foot, had not something lucky happened.

The luggage of the passengers for the next flight was being loaded into the hold of the aircraft, and one of the loaders put down a suitcase while he went to help with another heavier piece of luggage. He put it down right beside the wheel.

"Curious," said Siegfried. "What is this thing?" and slowly he slid up off the ground and onto the suitcase.

Chance is a funny thing, and Siegfried could not have known that this suitcase belonged to a man called Steven Nail, who was flying to America on business. But the warm leather felt comfortable under his foot, and he settled himself just above a row of letters stamped into the side of the case, which read:

S. NAIL

Chapter Two

You'd hardly believe this, but when the baggage handler came back to pick up Steven Nail's leather suitcase, a trolley arrived beside the aircraft. On it were a number of pieces of baggage, amongst which was a strange-looking bag, made of a sort of grey canvas, and sealed and indeed clamped at its neck. It was a diplomatic bag. On it were two labels.

One read:

BY HAND OF PILOT

The other said:

HM'S AMBASSADOR
FLOOR 5
BRITISH EMBASSY
WASHINGTON DC
USA

The baggage handler picked up Mr
Nail's suitcase to put it on the trolley. He
dumped it down so hard that Siegfried fell
off, landing on the diplomatic bag.

Now all the luggage was loaded into the hold of the aircraft, except of course the one that said BY HAND OF PILOT, which was taken to the cockpit. And so when the jumbo jet took off from the airport, neither the pilot nor the co-pilot knew that, stuck on the clamped neck of the diplomatic bag beside them, was a British snail who, though he did not know it, was travelling to America.

Siegfried stayed stock-still during the eight-hour journey across the Atlantic. Something told him he was having an adventure. Though the leather of Mr Nail's suitcase had been comfortable, he preferred the diplomatic bag. When the aircraft landed at the airport at Washington, he made sure that he was stuck on tight to the metal clamp round the neck of the bag. The clamp was snail-coloured, and it would have taken a very sharp eye to detect Siegfried. Certainly the messenger sent to collect the diplomatic bag noticed nothing, nor, after the car journey which took it to the British Embassy, did anyone on the staff. Except for one person, the British Ambassador himself.

Sir Robin Bracken was a tall, dark, handsome man, with smooth black hair and bushy black eyebrows, underneath which was a pair of extremely sharp eyes.

When he entered his office that morning, his secretary said, "A bag has arrived, Your Excellency," and she put it down on his desk.

Sir Robin reached out to break the seals and undo the clamp, when he suddenly spotted the stowaway. "Well I'll be blowed!" he said, and he pointed to Siegfried. The secretary, who was short-sighted, peered at the snail through her thick spectacles and let out a little scream of alarm.

"Oh!" she cried. "It looks like an explosive device! Oh sir, the bag is booby-trapped, don't touch it, please. I'll sound the alarm for the security people!"

"Do not do so foolish a thing," said the Ambassador, and, very gently, he detached Siegfried from his resting place and put him down on the desk.

"Explosive device my foot!" he said, laughing, as Siegfried moved off on his own foot, very slowly, leaving a trail of slime on the polished surface. "This is a gastropod mollusc."

"Oh Sir Robin, whatever does that mean?" asked the bewildered secretary.

"Well, a mollusc is something with a soft body and a hard shell, and 'gastropod' means that it travels on its foot, as it is doing now."

"But however did it get on the diplomatic bag?"

"If only you could tell us, old chap," said Sir Robin Bracken gently to Siegfried.

"My guess is that you are a stowaway from Britain, though I can't think how you boarded the aeroplane."

Just for a bit of fun, he thought, I'll take this British snail and introduce him to the President of the United States of America. I'm sure he'd like to meet so bold an adventurer.

Chapter Three

How lucky Siegfried was to have met Sir
Robin Bracken, for he was a most
knowledgeable man. Not only was he a
diplomat, he was also a keen naturalist, and
he knew quite a bit about *Helix Pomatia*,
the Common Snail.

He knew that, as well as
its protective shell and its
slimy foot that pulsed and
thus drove it along, it also
had a pair of eyes and a
pair of mouths, on top of its
head. He knew too that those
mouths would be longing for food
after such a journey, and so he put

Siegfried into the pot of a large ornamental plant that stood on his office windowsill. On the earth in which the plant grew was some old leaf-matter, which snails, he knew, very much liked.

"There you are, old chap," said Sir Robin to Siegfried. "You have a jolly good feed and then we'll pay a call on Mr President at the White House."

That afternoon, when the Ambassador had had enough of working at his desk and the snail, he thought, should have satisfied his hunger, he picked Siegfried up, very gently, and popped him into a little pillbox which he put in the pocket of his well-tailored suit.

"Please call my car," he said to his secretary. "I'll be at the White House if you want me."

"Sir Robin!" cried the President as the British Ambassador was shown in. "Good to see ya! How're ya doin'?"

"I'm very well, thank you, Mr President," replied the Ambassador as they shook hands.

"Gee, ain't it hot!" said the President as they sat down at the handsome table that stood in the centre of the Oval Office.

"Remarkably warm indeed," said Sir Robin. "You must be worried about pollution."

"Don't know about pollution," replied the President. "It's all these particles floating about in the atmosphere."

"Ah yes. Quite. Toxic particles, you mean, like pesticides?"

"Don't know about pesticides. I'm talking about all the stuff farmers use for killing pests."

"Quite so. And then there's the overproduction of carbon dioxide."

"Sure, sure, Sir Robin, you put your finger on it. Now then, what can I do for you? No trouble at home, I hope? How's my friend the Prime Minister?"

"The Prime Minister is very well, thank you, Mr President," replied the Ambassador. "I am the bearer of certain messages from him," and he put a hand in his breast-pocket and took out some papers. When the two men had discussed them, Sir Robin suddenly remembered what was in another pocket of his suit. He took out the pillbox, removed its lid, lifted Siegfried out, and placed him carefully upon the table. "I thought this might interest you."

The President of the United States looked totally bewildered. "Jiminy Crickets!" he said. "It's a snail! Why, we got millions of the critters in America."

"But this is a British snail," said Sir Robin Bracken.

The President stretched out a hand and scratched Siegfried's shell. "Hey, feller," he said. "Lucky for you I ain't a Frenchman. They eat snails."

Perhaps it was the sound of the President's voice, perhaps it was the scratching of the Presidential finger, but Siegfried now began to move across the table, not towards the Englishman but towards the American.

"But I still can't figure," said Mr President, "why you've brought the little feller along."

"It seemed to me," said Sir Robin, "that you might be interested in this particular snail, Mr President. He's quite an adventurer. He stowed away on a flight from Britain, attached to a diplomatic bag. He is an immigrant, following in the footsteps of all those millions of people who have come from every part of the world to make their homes here in America."

By now Siegfried had slid close to the side of the table at which the President was sitting. As usual he spoke his thoughts out loud – but not loudly enough for human ears to hear.

"I don't know who these people are," he said, "but they're doing an awful lot of talking," and, slowly and slimily, he crawled on to the President's hand.

"Aw gee!" said Mr President. "He kinda likes me!"

Chapter Four

"Possibly," said Sir Robin, "he recognizes a kindred spirit."

The President looked not best pleased. "You British!" he said. "You gotta mighty strange sense of humour. You're saying I'm as slow as this snail?"

"Certainly not, Mr President," said the Ambassador. "We all know how quick-thinking and how quick-acting you are. Though of course there is that old saying 'More haste, less speed'. No, no, I simply meant that you have much in common with the creature sitting on your hand. For example, he is adventurous, as you are."

The President looked better pleased.

"And to have undertaken so long a journey, he must be brave, as you are."

The President looked even more pleased.

"And thirdly," went on Sir Robin, "he is above all determined. This, something tells me, is a most determined snail, just as you, as everyone knows, are a most determined man, who will lead America to great things."

The President beamed.

After all, said the Ambassador to himself, flattery is one of the tools of a diplomat.

Thanks to my good old snail, I may improve my standing with the most powerful man on earth.

"Why, thanks, Sir Robin!" said the President. "Mighty nice of you to be so complimentary. Yes, there's a whole bunch of stuff to do, but we'll stick at it."

"I'm sure you will, Mr President," said the Ambassador.

"Just like this little feller's sticking to me," said the President, and with his right hand he removed Siegfried from his left one and placed him back on the table.

"What are you up to?" said Siegfried. "I'd just got nice and comfortable there. Oh well, if you don't want me, I'll go back to my friend," and he set off, slowly of course, across the table towards the British Ambassador.

The President stood up. "Mighty nice of you to bring that snail along, Sir Robin," he said. "Waddya going to do with him?"

"I'm not sure, Mr President," replied Sir Robin. "I'll have to find out which state he plans to settle in."

"You Brits!" laughed the President. "Darned if I know when you're joking! But I'll have to let you go now, Sir Robin – I gotta meet with the French Ambassador."

"Of course," said Sir Robin Bracken, and he produced his pillbox and popped Siegfried in.

Back at the British Embassy, the Ambassador took the pillbox from his pocket and addressed Siegfried. "What am I going to do with you, old chap?" he said. "I can't just turn you loose."

Siegfried the adventurer was curious too. "What are you going to do with me?" he asked, but of course there was no answer.

"One thing's certain," said Sir Robin. "I'm not just going to let you go wandering about in Washington DC, however much you wanted to come to America in the first place. Anything might happen to you. I must keep you safe until I've decided what to do. Now let me think, what do snails need?"

He called his secretary and asked her, much to her puzzlement, to find him a plastic sandwich box, a lettuce, an apple, a cucumber and some gravel.

Sir Robin punched holes in the lid of the box (so that the snail would be able to breathe), lined the bottom of it with the gravel, over which he poured some water (snails like damp places) and put into the box a lettuce leaf, a slice of apple and another of cucumber, and, finally, Siegfried.

"What d'you think of that, old chap?" he said, and put the lid on.

"I say, this is nice!" said Siegfried, and eagerly he began to eat, scraping the food with the rough file-like tongues of his two mouths. With one of his two eyes he looked up and saw the face of the Ambassador peering down at him through the plastic lid.

"Cheers!" said Siegfried, with both his mouths full.

Chapter Five

That evening the Ambassador said to his wife, "By the way, I've got a new pet."

"Not a dog, I hope," said Lady Bracken, "or there'll be all that quarantine business when we go home."

"No, not a dog."

"What then?"

"A snail."

"Oh Robin!" said his wife. "The British Ambassador keeping a pet snail! What on earth would the Foreign Office say if they knew?"

"They may well know, Sally," said Sir
Robin. "I have already introduced my snail
to the President."

"Honestly!" cried Lady Bracken. "He'll
think you're a nutter!"

"On the contrary. He took rather a shine
to the little chap."

"Where is he now?"

"Who, the President?"

"No, the snail."

"In my office. In a large, airy sandwich
box, lined with damp gravel."

"Have you fed him?"

"Of course. Lettuce, apple and cucumber. He wants for nothing."

Lady Bracken looked thoughtful. "I wouldn't be too sure about that, Robin," she said.

"What d'you mean?"

"Well, picture yourself – in a large comfortable apartment with wall-to-wall carpeting and lots of good food. Isn't there something missing?"

"Like what, Sally?"

"Like me."

"Oh. I see what you mean. My snail needs a partner."

"Well," said the Ambassador's wife, "why not put another snail in with him? Or her. Even if it wasn't boy and girl, but two boys or two girls, it'd be company."

"Sally," said Sir Robin, "what a brilliant idea. I'll go and find one now."

When the Ambassador entered his office the following morning, he went immediately to the sandwich box, on one wall of which Siegfried was firmly stuck by his big slimy foot. Sir Robin removed the lid.

"How are you, old chap?" he asked. "Sleep well?"

"Some people," Siegfried said, "never give one a moment's peace."

"I have a surprise for you," said the Ambassador, and he took the pillbox from his pocket, removed the lid and carefully took out another snail, which he put into the sandwich box.

It was a tiny bit smaller than Siegfried and a different colour. Siegfried's shell was blotchy – black with grey patches. The newcomer's shell was honey-coloured. Sir Robin had chosen it for this reason. Confident, somehow, that Siegfried was male, he saw the other as a dishy blonde.

"I've brought you a wife," he said. "I hope."

Throughout that working day he kept getting up to have a look in the sandwich box, but nothing seemed to be happening. Siegfried was still stuck to the wall, while the blonde was busy with a lettuce leaf.

As the Ambassador was about to leave his office at the end of the day, the telephone rang.

"Hullo," he said.

"Sir Robin?"

"Yes."

"It's the President here. I've been thinking about that snail of yours. How is the little feller?"

"Very well, thank you, Mr President."

38

"Has he told you yet which state he plans to settle in?"

"Er, no, not yet."

"When he does," said the President, "let me know, will ya?" and he rang off, but not before Sir Robin heard great snorts of laughter.

The Ambassador took a last look in the sandwich box but the two snails were no nearer to one another. "Come on, old chap," he said to his snail. "Aren't you going to make friends?"

I know what state I want my chap to settle in, he thought, and that's the state of matrimony.

Chapter Six

Later that evening in the British Embassy, the Ambassador's office was pleasantly dark. Pleasant, that is, for snails, who are most active at night.

"I'm hungry," said Siegfried. "I fancy some of that cucumber," and he flexed his foot and began to slide down the wall of the sandwich box. His mind on food, he did not look where he was going and suddenly bumped into something hard, something, he thought, that felt like the shell of a snail.

Drawing back a little, he poked out one

of his two telescopic eyes and saw that there was indeed another snail in the sandwich box. Cheek! he thought. Who invited him? Or her?

"What the dickens are you doing in here?" he asked.

The other snail turned to face him. "If it's any business of yours, buddy," it said, "I'm eating cucumber."

"It most certainly *is* my business," said Siegfried. "You're in my box and it's my cucumber."

"Gee whiz!" said the other. "You sound angry. But I like your voice. It's different. Where are you from?"

"Britain," said Siegfried.

"Britain! Howja get to Washington?"

"I flew."

"You flew?"

"Yes. In an aeroplane."

"My! How romantic!"

Three things now occurred to Siegfried.
One, that it was good to have someone to
talk to. Two, that he also liked the sound of
the other's voice. Three, was he a boy or
was she a girl?

Politeness costs nothing, he thought.

"I must beg your pardon," he said.

"Whatever for?"

"For speaking so rudely to you. Please
help yourself to some more cucumber. I'll
be quite happy with the apple."

Then there was quite a long silence while both snails fed.

After some time the blonde stranger said to Siegfried, "So you're British?"

"I am indeed."

"Waddya know! I've never met a British snail in my whole life."

"Actually, I've never met an American one. By the way, my name is Siegfried."

"Siegfried. That's a name for a guy, I guess. You're a male snail?"

"Yes."

Now's the moment, Siegfried thought. I'll ask what he, or she, is called, and the name should give it away. His eyes were out on stalks and he crossed them for luck.

"What are you called, may I ask?" he said.

"My name is Peggy-Sue."

Siegfried uncrossed his eyes. "That's awfully pretty," he said.

"Why, thank you, sir," said Peggy-Sue, and they both settled down again to eat.

When dawn came and the light flooded into the Ambassador's office, the two snails looked at one another.

He's handsome, thought Peggy-Sue, and Siegfried said to himself, "Gosh! She's a dishy blonde!"

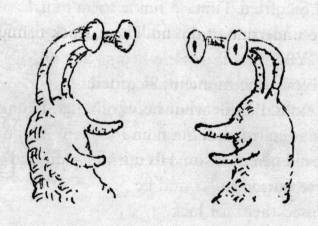

Later, the Ambassador came into his office
and made straight for the sandwich box.
He took off the lid and looked inside to see
bits of lettuce and apple and cucumber but
no snails!

Oh no! he thought. They've escaped.
Then an idea struck him and he looked on
the underside of the lid. There, stuck firmly
to it by their feet, were Peggy-Sue and
Siegfried, their shells just touching.

Sir Robin heaved a sigh of relief. Thank
Heavens, he thought. The President would
have been ever so narked if my snail had
gone missing.

Chapter Seven

At lunch time the Ambassador left his office and made his way to his apartment. He was carrying the sandwich box, the two snails still firmly attached to the underside of its lid. He needed his wife's opinion.

"Oh Robin, you've brought your pet snail!" said Lady Bracken.

"Snails, Sally. Look!" said her husband, and he took off the lid of the box. "The dark one is mine. Did I tell you, he came from England by air, attached to a diplomatic bag?"

"A stowaway! My word, what an adventurer!"

"Yes indeed. The President was most impressed."

"And the other one's an American snail?"

"The blonde? Yes, she is. Well, if she is a she."

"They seem very chummy," said Lady Bracken.

"At least it appears they've become close friends," said the Ambassador. "I think – I hope – that mine's a boy and the blonde's a girl. But how shall we ever know?"

"There's only one thing to do. Wait and see if one of them lays eggs."

47

So Sir Robin waited. So keen had he become on his unusual pets that he kept them with him all the time, solemnly carrying the sandwich box to his office each morning and bringing it back to his apartment each evening.

Before long there was another phone call from the President.

"How's your snail, Sir Robin?"

"Very well, thank you, Mr President. I've actually got two snails now."

"Gee whiz! You got the little feller a wife?"

"To be honest, Mr President, I'm not sure of the sex of either of them."

"Aw gee, that's tough. Mebbe I can help. I'll get me an expert. Speak to you soon," said the President. "And have a nice day!"

That very afternoon another call came from someone at the White House to the British Embassy. Would Sir Robin Bracken bring his snails to the Oval Office at eleven o'clock the following morning?

"Crumbs!" said Lady Bracken when told of this. "Your snails are getting really important."

When Sir Robin entered the Oval Office next day, he was warmly greeted by the President and then introduced to a grey-haired man wearing spectacles, whose name, the President informed him, was August P. Sassafras.

"Now then, Sir Robin," said the President proudly, "August here is Professor of Gastropolysomething – heck of a long word – put me right, August."

"Gastropodology," said the Professor.

"Just so. At one of our major universities. There ain't much about snails he don't know."

Brilliant! thought the British Ambassador. Now we shall find out which is what. He removed the lid from the sandwich box.

Within, Siegfried and Peggy-Sue were still eating breakfast. Side by side they were tucking into a juicy slice of fresh pineapple.

The Professor picked up Siegfried. "*Helix Pomatia,*" he said. "The Common Snail."

"Lemme tell ya, August," said the President, "he ain't common. He's a Brit, that snail is, and he flew across the Atlantic to get here."

"But my problem, Professor," said Sir Robin, "is that I don't know the sex of either of these snails. I was hoping you'd be able to help."

Professor Sassafras put Siegfried back into the sandwich box and took out Peggy-Sue. "This one a Brit too?" he asked.

"No, no," said the Ambassador. "That's a Washington snail. I like to think that the dark one is male and the blonde one is a female. Could I be right?"

For a while the Professor examined each snail in turn. It was as well that he was not aware of their reaction.

"What's this wretched person doing?" said Siegfried. "I can't eat my breakfast in peace. Every time I settle down to the pineapple, he picks me up. I don't like it."

"Me neither, Siegfried," replied Peggy-Sue. "It fair gets on a girl's nerves."

Eventually Professor Sassafras put both snails into the box and stood back.

"Well, Professor?" said the Ambassador.

"Well, August?" said the President.

The Professor peered down at Siegfried and Peggy-Sue through his spectacles. Then he straightened up.

"Mr President," he said. "Right from my boyhood in Virginia I was taught always to tell the truth."

"Like George Washington," said the President. "He came from Virginia too, I think."

"What's more, I believe that honesty is the best policy."

"It is," said Sir Robin Bracken. "So – was I right?" He pointed to Siegfried. "Is this a male?" he asked, and then, pointing to Peggy-Sue, "Is this a female?"

There was a moment's silence.

"Gentlemen," said the Professor of Gastropodology, "I don't have the faintest idea. There's only one thing to do. Wait and see if one of them lays eggs."

Chapter Eight

The normally well-ordered mind of Sir Robin Bracken now became obsessed with one subject – snails' eggs. He had visited the public library and found a book on snails. One female, he read, could lay as many as forty eggs.

Somehow he managed not to neglect the duties of his high office, but he could not stop himself thinking, last thing at night, Will there be any eggs in the sandwich box tomorrow? As soon as he woke every

morning, he would hastily put on his
dressing-gown and slippers and hurry to
the bathroom, which is where Siegfried and
Peggy-Sue spent each night in their box.

The bathroom, the Ambassador thought,
should be the dampest room. So that the
snails might enjoy total darkness, unspoiled
by any form of light, he would cover them
up with a cloth each evening when he
went to say goodnight to them, as one
might put a cover over the cage of a parrot
or canary. By day he took them to his office,
and he also took a number of telephone calls
from the President, which usually went
something like this:

"Sir Robin!"

"Mr President?"

"Any eggs yet?"

"I fear not."

"Keep me in the picture, won't ya? You gotta get lucky some day. Remember, 'Hope springs eternal in the human breast', as some guy said, I dunno who."

"Alexander Pope," the Ambassador replied.

"No, I don't think it was the Pope – Shakespeare more likely. Anyway, the best of British luck to you."

Weeks passed with no sign of eggs. Perhaps they need a richer diet, thought Sir Robin, and he ordered exotic fruits like guava and mango and avocado pear, and unusual vegetables such as kohl-rabi and winter parsnip.

One evening the Ambassador returned to his private apartment, carrying the sandwich box of course, and looking, his wife thought, rather down in the mouth.

"What's the matter, Robin?" Lady Bracken asked. "You look as if you've lost a dollar and found a dime."

"The President just rang," said Sir Robin.

"Again? What did he say to make you look so depressed?"

"He said he'd been talking to that Professor of Gastropodology, August Sassafras. 'I've just had a word with August,' he said to me. 'Told him you weren't getting any eggs and d'you know what he said? He said he reckons both your snails are males.' I'd never thought of that, Sally."

My husband has a brilliant brain,

thought Lady Bracken to herself, yet he'd never thought of that.

"Why don't you just let them go, Robin?" she said. "Wouldn't they be happier?"

"No, no, they're very happy together, always side by side, eating or sleeping. That's why I still think they're a pair."

Depressed the Ambassador may have been that evening, but the following morning he came back from his inspection of the sandwich box grinning all over his face.

"Guess what, Sally," he said.

"Eggs?"

"Yes! Six of them, little tiny round things."

"Who laid them?"

"Why, the blonde, I imagine."

"You imagine, Robin, but you don't know for sure."

"Well no, I suppose not."

"There's only one way to find out," said Sally. "There'll probably be more eggs to come – you said they laid as many as forty – so get another sandwich box and separate your beloved snails. That way you'll find out who is the mummy."

"But they'll be unhappy apart."

"Not as unhappy as you will be, not knowing."

So the Ambassador sent out for a second sandwich box and some more gravel to line it with. He took off the lid of the first box and addressed the occupants.

"Now which of you shall I put in the new place?" he asked them. "There's only one way to decide," and he began "Eenie meenie minie mo . . ."

"Now what?" said Siegfried to Peggy-Sue. "I just want to be left alone to eat my—" But that was as far as he got, for the choice had fallen upon him.

"You'll like it in here, old chap," said Sir Robin as he put Siegfried into the new box.

"I've got a nice slice of pawpaw specially for you."

That afternoon, while the Ambassador was busy at his desk and Siegfried was busy eating pawpaw, Peggy-Sue was busy too. Who knows, perhaps she had only laid six eggs before because of the lack of privacy, but now, left alone, she proceeded to lay a great many more.

His day's work finished, Sir Robin went over to inspect his sandwich boxes. In one Siegfried, fully fed, was stuck to the side, motionless. In the other, Peggy-Sue was greedily tucking into a bit of avocado pear, and there beside her on the floor of the box was a mass of snail's eggs!

A suave and worldly diplomat Sir Robin Bracken may have been, but at this sight he

was as excited as a small boy
at Christmas. Feverishly, with
the aid of a magnifying
glass, he began to count
the eggs. Then he
telephoned his wife.

"She's done it!" he
shouted.

"Who's done what?" asked Lady
Bracken.

"The blonde! She's laid forty eggs!"

"Oh Robin, how splendid! I'll get the
champagne ready."

Then he telephoned the President. "I thought you might like to know, Mr President," he said, "that my snail is a father. His blonde wife from Washington has laid forty eggs."

"Holy mackerel!" cried the President. "This is great news, Sir Robin! Waddya know, there'll soon be forty little snails with a British poppa and an American momma!"

"Yes," said Sir Robin. "It is a fine example of that special relationship that exists between my country and yours."

Chapter Nine

Sir Robin took both the sandwich boxes up to his apartment. He somehow felt that the new mum would need peace and quiet after all that effort of egg-laying, so he left his adventurous snail on his own for the time being.

Lady Bracken was of course much impressed by the great number of eggs and the champagne was duly opened and a toast drunk to mother and children. Then the phone rang.

It was the White House.

"Sir Robin!"

"Mr President?"

"How are the new arrivals doing?"

"Fine, as far as I can tell."

"I've told my buddy the British Prime Minister about it."

"And what did he have to say?"

"Not a lot, Sir Robin. I was mighty disappointed. He didn't seem all that interested."

"Perhaps he had other things on his mind."

"Mebbe. I thought I'd tell him a joke, to cheer him up. I'll try it on you. Why did the snail cross the road?"

"To get to the other side?"

"No, no, that ain't funny."

"Well, why did the snail cross the road?"

"Because he saw a big sign that said SLOW."

"Very good, Mr President. May I try one on you?"

"Go right ahead."

"Which came first, the snail or the egg?"

"The snail of course. She's gotta lay the egg."

"But she must have hatched out of an egg."

"Well, I'll be doggoned. Reminds me though – I want to ask you a very special favour, Sir Robin."

"Whatever I can do for you, I will, Mr President," said the Ambassador.

"Then will you bring the mother snail and her babies over to the White House and let me have them?"

"You want them? For yourself?"

"No, for August Sassafras. I told him about the eggs and he's crazy to have them to study. We know the date they were laid and so he can find out exactly how long it takes for them to hatch into snails. No one's ever been quite certain."

"I see. So it will be a gastropodological breakthrough?"

"What? Oh yeah, sure. So will ya let him have them?"

"You don't want the male snail too?"

"Nah, August ain't interested in him. Just bring the momma and the kids."

Sir Robin felt relieved that he was not losing his adventurous snail. I do feel bad about taking away his girlfriend and his babies, he thought, but it's what the President wants.

"Certainly, Mr President," he said.

"Gee thanks, I'm mighty obliged to you."

The Ambassador put down the phone and took off the lid of the sandwich box on the side of which Siegfried was stuck.

"Don't worry, old chap," he said. "We'll stick together, you and I."

"For goodness' sake," said Siegfried. "Get my supper. I'm hungry – what are you thinking of? And put the cover on, it's too bright in here."

"What did the President want?" asked Lady Bracken.

"The blonde snail and the eggs. For the Professor of Gastropodology to study."

"And you said yes?"

"I thought it diplomatic," said her husband.

"You do realize, Robin," said Lady Bracken, "that at the end of this month we fly home on leave. What do you intend to do about the stow-away? You can't take him with you, you know. There's a law against bringing any old pet into the UK. He'll have to stay here until we return. I suppose your secretary could look after him. It's only a matter of feeding him, he doesn't need exercising."

"I shall miss him," the Ambassador said.

"Oh Robin, honestly, he's only a snail!"

He's not "only a snail", Sir Robin thought. He's my snail, my very own brave, curious, determined, adventurous snail, and I want him to come with us when we go.

Chapter Ten

The day came for the Brackens to fly home
on leave. As they got into the limousine
that was to take them to the airport, Lady
Bracken said to her husband, "I hope you
said 'Adieu!' to your precious snail?"

"I said 'Au revoir!' " replied Sir Robin.

These were indeed the words he'd used
when, early that morning, he had taken
Siegfried out of his sandwich box, and
popped the snail and a nice slice of melon

71

into another diplomatic bag, which he then sealed and clamped. This one also bore two labels. One read:

THE FOREIGN OFFICE
LONDON

The other said:

BY HAND OF THE BRITISH AMBASSADOR

Inside the bag, the feel of which was familiar to him, Siegfried tucked into the melon. Something told him he was having another adventure.

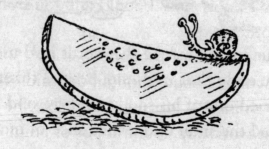

Back in London a car was waiting to take the Ambassador and his wife to their country home. There, while Lady Bracken was occupied with unpacking, Sir Robin quickly took Siegfried from the diplomatic bag and popped him into his pillbox.

"It's a tough choice for me, old chap," he said, "but I've decided to turn you loose. You're a British snail, after all, and with a bit of luck you'll find yourself another friend. It'll be nice for me, when we go back to the States, to know that you'll be living happily in my garden. I might even see you again, though I don't know how I could tell you from all the other snails."

He paused for thought.

"Wait a minute though," he said. "I've had an idea." Carrying the pillbox he went to his workshop, found a pot of paint –

Brilliant Red, it was – and carefully put a little blob of it on the top of Siegfried's shell.

"What are you up to now?" said Siegfried as Sir Robin carried him down the garden to a far corner where there was a fish-pond.

"I think this should do you fine, old chap," said the Ambassador. "It's nice and damp, and there are lots of cracks and crevices in between the stones for you to hide in." He took Siegfried out of the pillbox and put him down on the flagstones that surrounded the pond.

Sir Robin sat on a bench in the sunshine, watching as Siegfried flexed his foot and slid slowly and slimily away under that red-marked shell.

"I just hope you don't miss your blonde friend too much," Sir Robin called after him.

In the days and nights to come Siegfried was too busy exploring his new surroundings to think much about his American adventures. He was not lonely, for the Ambassador's garden was full of snails, but then there came a day when he met one exactly the same colour as Peggy-Sue.

Could it be her? he thought excitedly. Could she somehow have got here too? He slid up to the blonde snail.

"Peggy-Sue?" he asked. "Can you be my Peggy-Sue?"

"Push off, mate," replied the other snail. "My name's Fred, so get lost, unless you want a mouthful of slime!"

As Sir Robin Bracken's holiday neared its end, both he and his adventurous snail were unhappy. Search as he might, the Ambassador had never caught sight of a snail with a red mark on its back, and, try as he might, Siegfried found he could not get Peggy-Sue out of his mind.

But then, on the final morning of the Ambassador's leave, fortune smiled upon them both.

Waiting for a car to take them to the airport, Sir Robin had a last stroll down to the fish-pond. It was a damp morning and there were plenty of snails about, but they were ordinary common-or-garden ones. I don't expect I'll ever see my snail again, he thought sadly. I should have left him in

Washington. Then he'd have been waiting for me when we got back.

He turned to go up to the house, and there, on the path in front of him, was a snail with a red mark on its shell!

"The car's here, Robin!" Lady Bracken called.

"I'm coming!" shouted the Ambassador.

We're coming, he said to himself, and he picked up Siegfried and shoved him into the pocket of his jacket.

"It's nice and dark in here," said Siegfried as they flew across the Atlantic again, "but it's hot and I'm hungry. Ah well, it all comes of being adventurous, I suppose."

Once back at the British Embassy in Washington, Sir Robin went to his office. His secretary greeted him. She looked worried.

"What's the matter?" he asked her.

"Oh Sir Robin!" she said. "It's your pet snail. You must have left the lid off its box when you went on leave. It's gone!"

"Oh don't worry," the Ambassador replied. "I'll soon get another." He waited till she had left the room and then he took Siegfried from his jacket pocket and put him back in his sandwich box. He pulled some leaves off his pot plant and dropped them in. The phone rang.

"Sir Robin?"

"Mr President?"

"You had a good leave?"

"Yes, thank you."

"I got news for you. Your snail's eggs have hatched, August tells me. He's mighty obliged to you, and he says he doesn't want the momma any more. D'you want her back?"

"Oh yes please, Mr President! Oh my goodness, you've made my day! 'The lark's on the wing, The snail's on the thorn, God's in His heaven, All's right with the world!'"

"I ain't never gonna understand the Brits," said the President to himself as he put the phone down.

Sir Robin Bracken, the British Ambassador to the United States of America, never forgot the pure joy of the moment when he took the lid off a sandwich box in which was a black-and-grey specimen of *Helix Pomatia*, and put into it again a blonde snail of the same species.

Siegfried never forgot the pure joy of the moment when his two telescopic eyes focused once more upon his beloved.

"Oh Peggy-Sue!" he said. "You're back!"

"Yes, Siegfried dear. It's lovely to see you again. But what's that red mark on top of your shell?"

"Red mark?" said Siegfried. "Didn't know I had one."

"It's ever so attractive," she said.

"And so are you," said Siegfried the adventurous snail.

THE END